X   Greve, Meg, author.
006.754   Social Media and the
GRE   Internet   BER

5/2017

ST. MARY PARISH LIBRARY
FRANKLIN, LOUISIANA

SOCIAL MEDIA and the INTERNET

Written by Meg Greve

Content Consultant
Taylor K. Barton, LPC
School Counselor

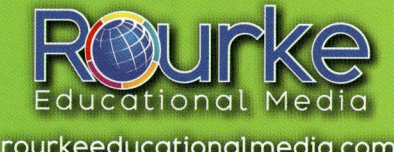

Rourke Educational Media
rourkeeducationalmedia.com

Scan for Related Titles and Teacher Resources

© 2014 Rourke Educational Media

All rights reserved. No part of this book may be reproduced or utilized in any form or by any means, electronic or mechanical including photocopying, recording, or by any information storage and retrieval system without permission in writing from the publisher.

www.rourkeeducationalmedia.com

PHOTO CREDITS: Cover: © Peathegee Inc; page 4: © VikramRaghuvanshi; page 5: © cogal; page 6: © skynesher; page 7: © kali9; page 8: © sturti; page 9: © German; page 10: © SpiffyJ; page 11: © Dusan Jankovic; page 12: © Alejandro Rivera; page 13 © Hocus Focus Studio; page 15: © Igor Mojzes; page 16: © fstop123; page 17: © kali9; page 18: © Lisa Thornberg; page © Steve Debenport; page 20: © Sadeugra; page 21: © dem10; page 22: © fstop123

Edited by Precious McKenzie

Cover and Interior Design by Tara Raymo

Library of Congress PCN Data

Social Media and the Internet / Meg Greve
(Social Skills)
ISBN 978-1-62169-907-1 (hard cover) (alk. paper)
ISBN 978-1-62169-802-9 (soft cover)
ISBN 978-1-62717-013-0 (e-Book)
Library of Congress Control Number: 2013937302

Rourke Educational Media
Printed in the United States of America,
North Mankato, Minnesota

rourkeeducationalmedia.com
customersevice@rourkeeducationalmedia.com • PO Box 643328 Vero Beach, Florida 32964

TABLE OF CONTENTS

Technology: Tool or Toy? 4

Staying Safe 8

Getting Smart 12

Having Fun 18

Glossary 23

Index 24

Websites to Visit 24

About the Author 24

Technology: Tool or Toy?

Technology can be anything from a laptop, to a smartphone, or even a calculator. We use technology every day to complete many of our jobs. Without technology, communicating, learning, and playing would be very different.

Tech Wise Tip

Make sure that all of your technology is connected. It makes it much easier for you to find a favorite song or video if you sync your technology.

Technology is an important tool we need for school and home. We use computers to do homework and smartphones to text our parents. Technology keeps us in touch with people who live far away. We can use a video chat program on our computers to see and talk to grandparents who live far away.

Technology has also become one of the most important toys in our lives. It allows us to watch movies from anywhere, play any song we want to hear, read our favorite books, and destroy alien ships from the comfort of our couches.

You're using technology as a tool for school when you e-mail your teacher about a homework question or you go online to research topics for a science project.

Tech Wise Tip

Get a waterproof cover for your favorite mp3 player. Dropping it once in a puddle or the pool can ruin it.

Because technology is a tool and a toy, the lines of safety and **appropriate** use can become confused. That is why you need to treat technology with the respect it deserves and follow all of the safety rules.

STAYING SAFE

Would you ever leave your front door wide open when you are going to bed? Would you ever share your most private thoughts with the local newspaper so they can print them? No? Well, if you are not careful online, you could very well be doing all of those things and worse.

Always keep safety in mind when you are using technology. Follow some simple rules and technology will help, not hurt, you!

Rule #1

Never share your **password** with anyone but your parents. Your password is the key to all of your secrets, and probably some of your parents' private information as well. With your password, anyone can do anything they want to with your technology and secrets.

Rule #2

Use a variety of letters and numbers for your password. Never make your password easy to figure out. It is also a good idea to change your password every once in awhile.

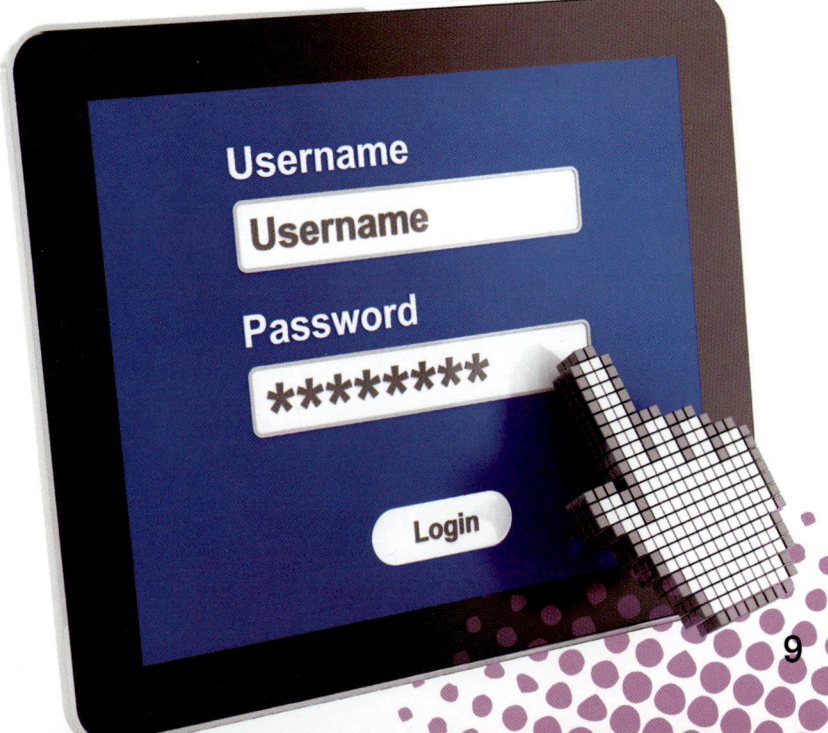

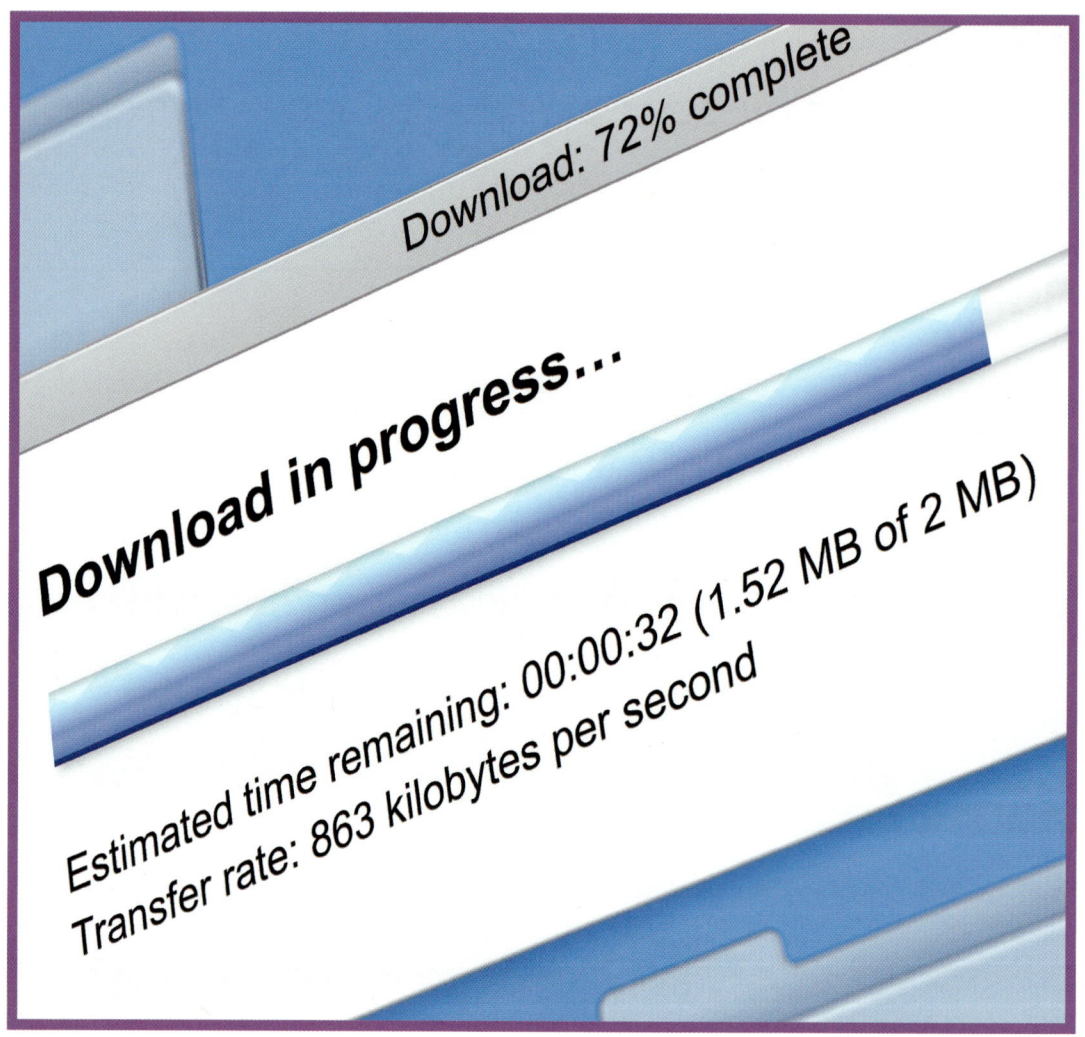

Rule #3

Be sure you know what you are downloading. If an offer is too good to be true, it probably is. Many **pop-up** windows will offer prizes for contests. This is a way for criminals to go **phishing** for personal information about you and your family. This is also a very easy way for **hackers** to infect your computer or smartphone with a **virus**.

Tech Wise Tip

Be careful when you reply to e-mails or texts. Pay attention to the people you are sending messages to. Never send a message that says anything you wouldn't say in person. Once you send it, you can never take the message back.

Rule #4

Be careful when someone e-mails a link to you. E-mail addresses are easy for criminals to steal and one click on a link can destroy your computer. If an e-mail from a friend seems weird or unusual, do not click on it. Delete it immediately and contact your friend about it.

GETTING SMART

Just a few short years ago, students had to go to the library and search for the perfect book or encyclopedia to research a topic. If the book was checked out, the student was out of luck. Technology has changed all of that. Now the library is at your fingertips on your computer or tablet.

Tech Wise Tip

Many public libraries have e-books you can borrow, not buy. This is a great way to get smart and save money!

When doing your homework or researching a project, the easiest first step is to use a search engine such as Google or Bing to help you find what you need. When looking for a specific topic, type in keywords. For example, if you are trying to learn about the pyramids in Egypt, type in *pyramids Egypt history*. It is not a good idea to type in a complete sentence, like I *want to learn about the pyramids in Egypt*. The smaller, less important words might limit what you are looking for.

Tech Wise Tip

When searching online for information, you need to make sure a grown-up knows what you are doing. Sometimes websites appear that are not okay for children. A good trick for getting better choices is to add the word *kids* or *for kids* at the end of your search. Usually more kid-friendly website choices will appear first.

Technology is also a great tool students use to study or memorize basic facts. There are many free websites that offer free flashcard makers or flashcard games. There are also a variety of educational websites that have games you can play to help you practice math facts, spelling, reading, and science.

There are also many free apps available that allow you to record your voice for playback or uploading. These apps are perfect when you need to hear how you sound when public speaking.

Look for software or **apps** that will help you create great presentations. There are many websites that allow you to design your presentation and upload photos or video and music clips to make a more interesting project.

HAVING FUN

The best part about technology is the fun you can have with it. Smartphones and tablets give you a chance to connect with friends and family in many ways.

Facebook and Instagram are two very popular social **networking** sites. Both give users the chance to share their thoughts, photos, or videos with others. On Facebook, you can create your own timeline and profile page. Friends and family can comment on your thoughts and pictures. On Instagram, you can post pictures, and then others can comment on or like your pictures.

Tech Wise Tip

Never post information on social media sites about when you are going on vacation. Criminals have been known to use social media sites to find homes to break into.

Be careful with the people you communicate with on these sites. People may not really be who they say they are. Remember that real friendships and relationships include time spent in person.

Tech Wise Tip

There are many social networking sites, such as Facebook and Instagram. These sites have very strict age requirements that must be followed. You must be at least 13 years of age or older to join. As with any technology, it is a privilege to use it and you must respect the rules.

Technology will always be a part of your life. The key is to recognize how to use it safely and responsibly. Use it as a tool or a toy, just be sure to be careful.

GLOSSARY

appropriate (uh-PROH-pree-uht): something that is right for you

apps (APPS): short for applications, software that allows you to play games or perform a task with your computer, tablet, or smartphone

hackers (HAK-urs): people who get into your computer files illegally

networking (NET-wurk-ing): getting together with other people online for the purpose of sharing friendships or information

password (PASS-wurd): a series of letters and numbers that allow you to lock others out of your technology

phishing (FISH-ing): tricking others to reveal personal information online

pop-up (POP-UP): a window that opens within a website suddenly, usually in the form of an advertisement

virus (VYE-ruhss): a computer program that infects and damages a technology device

INDEX

apps   17
criminals   10, 11
e-mail(s)   6, 11
laptop   4
password   9

pictures   19
research   6, 12
search engine   14
smartphone(s)   4, 6, 10, 18

WEBSITES TO VISIT

www.fbi.gov/fun-games/kids/kids-safety
www.safekids.com/kids-rules-for-online-safety
www.nypl.org/help/about-nypl/legal-notices/internet-safety-tips

ABOUT THE AUTHOR

Meg Greve lives in Chicago with her two children, Madison and William and her husband Tom. Madison and William love to teach their parents all about technology and how to use their devices!